P9-CDA-905

Miriam "Ma" Ferguson

First Woman Governor of Texas

Miriam "Ma" Ferguson

First Woman Governor of Texas

Judy Alter

Illustrated by Patrick Messersmith

McMurry University
Abilene, Texas

Library of Congress Cataloging-in-Publication Data

Alter, Judy, 1938-

Miriam "Ma" Ferguson : first woman governor of Texas / Judy Alter; illustrated by Patrick Messersmith.

p. cm.–(Stars of Texas series)

Includes bibliographical references and index.

ISBN-13: 978-1-933337-01-2 (hardcover: alk. paper)

ISBN-10: 1-933337-01-X (hardcover: alk. paper) 1. Ferguson, Miriam Amanda, 1875-1961—Juvenile literature. 2. Women governors—Texas—Biography—Juvenile literature. 3. Governors—Texas—Biography—Juvenile literature. 4. Texas—Politics and government—1865-1950—Juvenile literature. I. Messersmith, Patrick, ill. II. Title. III. Series.

F391.4.F47A45 2006
976.4'06092—dc22

2005032779

State House Press
McMurry Station, Box 637
Abilene, TX 79697-0637

Distributed by the Texas A&M University Press Consortium
(800) 826-8911 • www.tamu.edu/upress

Printed in the United States of America

ISBN-13: 978-1-933337-01-2
ISBN-10: 1-933337-01-X

Book designed by Rosenbohm Graphic Design

The Stars of Texas Series

Other books in this series include:

Mirabeau B. Lamar: Second President of Texas
Henrietta King: Rancher and Philanthropist

Free workbooks available on-line at
www.tamu.edu/upress/MCWHINEY/mcgen.html

Contents

Chapter 1

INTRODUCTION

*****

In the late twentieth century, women were prominent in politics nationally and in Texas. The Lone Star State saw Governor Ann Richards serve from 1991 until 1995. Kay Bailey Hutchison was elected to the United States Senate in 1993, the first woman to represent Texas in the Senate. Several women represented the state in the United States House of Representatives, and major cities have or have had women mayors.

Things were different in the 1920s. The State of Texas ratified the Nineteenth Amendment to the United States Constitution in 1920. That amendment gave women the right to vote and hold public office for the first time. Most women in Texas were not interested in politics. They wanted to stay at home and tend to their families.

Miriam Amanda Ferguson would also have liked to stay at home, but in 1924 she was elected governor of Texas. She was the first woman governor elected in the United States, but not the first woman to serve as governor.

Miriam Ferguson was one of six children of a well-to-do farmer. All the children were sheltered and given every opportunity, including education. Miriam was better educated than many young women of her day. She had been trained in manners and the proper way to do things.

A quiet, private person, she was a devout Christian who considered swearing and drinking sins. All she really wanted to do was to stay home in her big, comfortable house in Temple, Texas, take care of her husband, raise her two daughters, and tend to her flower garden.

After a long courtship, Miriam married Jim Ferguson. He was distantly related to Miriam by marriage. His widowed mother raised him after his father was killed. Jim and his mother were poor.

While Miriam liked to stay at home, Jim was out meeting people, making deals, always looking for the next opportunity. He was explosive and emotional, where Miriam was quiet and reserved. Jim would use tricks and jokes to win his political battles. Miriam loved to hear about his political tricks, but she mostly stayed out of them.

Jim Ferguson served two terms as governor of Texas. During his second term, in 1917, he was impeached for misusing his powers as governor. He was the first Texas governor to be impeached. The impeachment meant that he could not run again for public office,

Miriam Ferguson was not the first woman sworn in as a governor in the United States. Governor Nellie Ross of Wyoming was sworn in two weeks before Governor Ferguson. Her husband, Governor William B. Ross, had died in office.

so he decided his wife should be elected governor and he could continue to run the state.

Miriam agreed to run only to clear his name and restore her family's honor. In spite of all their differences, Miriam loved Jim Ferguson, and she thought he always knew best.

Miriam Ferguson served two terms as governor: from 1925 to 1927 and from 1933 to 1935 (a term was two years then instead of four as it is today). Historians have generally ignored Miriam or "Ma" Ferguson, as she came to be known, as one of Texas' less important governors. But even if historians don't think she is significant, Mrs. Ferguson has gone down in Texas folklore.

Everyone in Texas knows who Ma Ferguson was and hails her as the first woman governor.

Texas is the only state to elect two women governors—Miriam Ferguson and Ann Richards (1991-1995).

Chapter 2

An Idyllic Childhood

*****

Miriam Amanda Ferguson was raised on a farm in Central Texas near the town of Belton. At first her parents, Joseph Wallace and Eliza Garrison Wallace, raised their children in a five-room log house on Joseph's father's farm. Separate buildings held kitchen, dining room, store rooms, and servants' quarters. They were not poor farmers. Joseph Wallace saved enough to buy his father's farm. He grew cotton and raised cattle.

Miriam was born June 13, 1875, the third child in the Wallace family and the first girl. Because she had asthma, the family thought she was delicate and pampered her.

A black nanny raised her to be a southern lady and taught her to always behave in a ladylike fashion. "A whistling women and a crowing hen will never come to a good end," the nanny told her.

Miriam grew up as a very sheltered child who was not particularly independent.

Joseph wanted his children to have a good education. He had not spent much time in school himself. When he built a new, larger house, he located it near a school. Miriam attended Center Lake School for a while, but her father thought the education was not good enough. When she was thirteen, she and her two sisters—Susan Priscilla and Maggie Lee—had a tutor.

Joseph also wanted his children to be religious. The family attended church every Sunday, and the father led daily prayers in their home. Miriam was religious throughout her life.

Joseph Wallace did not send Miriam to the newly opened University of Texas because he thought she would be better educated and protected at a small woman's college.

***

Education

When Miriam was a teenager, she and two of her brothers were sent to live with an aunt in Salado so they could attend Salado College there. She studied scripture, prayers, and hymns, along with grammar, arithmetic, Latin, geography, penmanship, Greek, American history, and bookkeeping. Miriam liked learning and was a good student.

After Salado College, Miriam enrolled in Baylor Female College in Belton. She was nineteen. She recalled later that the meals were very plain, often just vegetables and gravy. Her father frequently sent candy and fruit and other treats from home. Miriam attended the school from 1894 until 1897 and then returned home.

Back on the farm, Miriam helped in the kitchen or in the fields. But she thought of herself as special—the educated and pampered daughter of a wealthy farmer, a girl whose family adored her. Home was the most comfortable place she could imagine, and she had no wish to leave her family.

Most young women her age wanted to have suitors, or boyfriends, to marry and start their own families. Miriam wasn't much interested in the men who came to call. And most of all she was not interested in Jim Ferguson.

Jim Ferguson, some four years older than she, was a neighbor. His father had been a circuit-riding preacher known as "The Fighting Parson" because he once challenged a parishioner to a fight. One day he scolded a member of his parish for not listening to his sermon. The legend is that the parishioner shot him.

Jim's widowed mother worked hard to raise her children. Jim's Uncle Wesley had been married to Miriam's mother before he died. Wesley Ferguson had caused a scandal by fighting for the Union during the Civil War.

Ouida Ferguson Nalle, daughter of Jim and Miriam, wrote that Texans are all kin, shaped by the air they breathe, the land they live on. She believed this explained her parents' attraction to each other and their strong love for their state. They both loved Texas, particularly Central Texas. Because Jim and Miriam were both from farming country, in politics they were always looking out for the farmers.

But whereas Miriam was educated and refined, Jim was rough around the edges. He was big and loud. He had worked in the fields as a young boy to help his widowed mother. He attended Salado College but then disappeared for two years. Later it turned out he had worked in restaurants, on railroads, even in gold mines. Around

Belton, he was known for his temper and also for the wild stories he told of his experiences out west. He was not a churchgoer.

***

Courtship

Miriam did not think this poor young man with a widowed mother would ever be able to give her all the comforts that she enjoyed in her father's home. She was horrified that Jim did not go to church and was against prohibition, although he himself did not drink. He believed everyone should decide individually on the drinking of alcoholic beverages.

When Jim Ferguson began to call on Miriam, he was reading law, preparing for a career as a lawyer. He really wanted to be in politics. Jim was a Populist. He

The Populist Party believed that people without influence, such as poor farmers, must stand and fight for their rights. They thought that government had an obligation to protect the poor, especially from the rich.

wanted to protect the poor people from the rich; he claimed the rich would cheat them and take their money. He also believed Texans should run Texas and was against immigration. He talked to Miriam about politics.

Miriam liked having Jim Ferguson come to call and she liked listening to him. She just didn't want to marry him.

Jim Ferguson knew that he would have to prove to Miriam that he could provide a life as comfortable as that her father had provided for her. He passed the bar and became a lawyer in 1897. Miriam was pleased that he had passed the bar, but when Jim proposed, she turned him down. When he had new offices, with his name etched on the glass, he proposed again. She said no again.

The committee who examined Jim during his bar examination was made up of friends of his father. They sent the young candidate out for whiskey and then raised their glasses in toasts to his father. They did not ask him any questions.

In January 1898, Miriam's father took a load of cattle to Kansas City for slaughter in mid-winter. His family warned him of the cold and danger, but he was determined. He said only an owner would ride in the car with the cattle and see that they were fed and watered. He returned home terribly sick from meningitis and died within days. Joseph Wallace left cash, land, and stock. Miriam's mother, not knowing what to do, consulted Jim. Jim Ferguson became the family's protector.

Chapter 3

Marriage, Children . . . and Politics

*****

Jim Ferguson finally got Miriam to agree to marriage. Both of their mothers approved, and Miriam may have been more inclined to marriage since she had lost her father. Jim needed a wife to advance his career because a man without a wife was not taken seriously in politics.

They were married on December 31, 1899, in a small wedding in the parlor of Mrs. Wallace's home, the large farmhouse where Miriam had been so happy. She was twenty-four; Jim was twenty-eight. Pictures of her as a young wife show a moderately pretty, solemn-looking young woman with her brown hair in a roll framing her face.

Mrs. Wallace built them a red cottage. Miriam loved the cottage and its gardens, where she worked when her asthma would let her. Jim knew that his bride was used to having household help, so he hired a cook and someone to tend their yard. Miriam was not strong enough to do the hard yard work all by herself, and Jim did not have the time or the interest.

Miriam was soon expecting their first child. To her surprise, she found that she liked marriage. Her days were not all that different than they had been in the family farmhouse. She spent her time gardening, resting, and reading, and she had Jim for company at meals and in the evenings. She rarely left her house and saw very few people. Her neighbors in Belton thought she was a recluse.

Their first child, Ouida, was born November 22, 1900. The second daughter, Dorrace, arrived in 1903. Miriam always said that

Ouida was Jim's child because even as an infant she was excitable and emotional. Dorrace, quiet and calm, was more like Miriam.

When fire burned a neighbor's house in Temple, Miriam was afraid it would spread to her house, but fortunately it did not. She took in the neighbors until they could find a place to stay.

Ouida recalled that Dorrace's birth shut out both herself and her father, and the two became closer because of her mother's attention to the younger daughter. Ouida also recalled a happy childhood, with a close family and a patient father. Ouida wanted to be a banker like her father, but her mother made it clear that ladies did not enter banking.

Ouida quoted her mother as having said she had two daughters, one who was a perfect lady and the other a sociable dog. Later in life, during Miriam and Jim's political battles, Ouida was one of their strongest supporters.

***

From Belton to Temple

Jim had established a bank in Belton, but his ambition soon outgrew that small town. He sold the bank and, with a partner, bought another bank in the nearby larger city of Temple.

Miriam said she was not moving herself or her babies from the cottage, so Jim commuted. He went to Temple in the mornings and returned to Belton at night. This difficult schedule was hard on him. His bank was doing very well, and he knew the family needed to live in Temple.

Jim bought a lot in Temple and contracted for a house to be built on it. Then he began to report construction progress to Miriam. He told her that if she did not join him in Temple, people would laugh at him. He told her the soil in Temple was better for gardening. Miriam said she was not moving to Temple, but she eventually did.

Their home in Temple was a large Victorian-style house, with decorative woodwork on its big verandah and a cupola. It was a comfortable house but not beautiful. Miriam often reminded her daughters, "This is your father's house."

Miriam planted a garden and began to feel at home. She joined the Daughters of the Republic of Texas and the United Daughters of the Confederacy, but she didn't socialize with Temple women as much as Jim wanted.

Miriam worried a great deal about keeping her family safe from disease and accidents. She was terrified of lightning. During storms both girls had to sleep at the foot of their parents' bed. Ouida remembered that they hated it. When Jim caught smallpox and Miriam developed appendicitis at the same time, Miriam was sure she would not live through the surgery. But the family did survive both illnesses.

Another time Jim's car caught on fire. The chauffeur was so badly burned he died three weeks later. After that, Jim would never learn to drive, so Miriam did all the driving for the family. To Miriam, her quiet life always seemed to be interrupted by something.

Ouida Ferguson Nalle insisted that her father ran for governor because he had conquered the world of banking in Central Texas. He was a success, but that was not enough for him. He needed a new adventure.

***

Governor Jim Ferguson

Jim was active in politics during their years in Temple, and campaigned for local candidates. Miriam thought Jim should stick to banking where he made money. But in 1914, he announced that he was going to run for governor. By then he was part owner of ten banks, managed Miriam's farm in Bell County, and had a ranch in Bosque County. Jim Ferguson was a busy and wealthy man.

During the campaign for governor, Jim Ferguson played up his poor background and assumed more country ways than were normal to him. He would appear before a crowd spitting tobacco and popping his suspenders. He wanted to be one of the people. He attacked his opponent's character, saying he was an alcoholic and deeply in debt. Ferguson won the election.

The Ferguson family arrived in Austin by private railroad car in January 1915. Jim was inaugurated on January 19, and the family moved into the governor's mansion.

Miriam's mother had recently died, and she was still in mourning. However, she knew she had to overcome her dislike of entertaining. Then she found out that the state did not pay for groceries. Jim's salary did not leave enough money for her to buy extra groceries, so Miriam did not entertain much. She was not used to having to watch her pennies, and she did not like it.

Miriam did occasionally invite the social ladies of Austin into the mansion, but it wasn't easy for her to be friendly. Other ladies misunderstood her quiet, reserved manner, and thought she was snobbish. She did not make many friends in Austin. When she hired a secretary to help her with the First Lady's duties, she was criticized even more.

The legislature voted to build a greenhouse for Miriam so that she could have fresh flowers for parties and receptions. She was very proud that her name was put in the cement doorstep to the greenhouse. When she returned to the mansion as governor, she was disappointed to see that someone had gotten rid of her name in the doorstep.

The Texas Legislature supported Jim. He had to deal with such problems as the Ku Klux Klan, prison reform, border security, and education for poor children.

The prohibition of alcohol was a major concern throughout the country, but Jim vetoed it in Texas. He and Miriam had serious disagreements about this. Jim expected citizens to drink responsibly, whereas Miriam approved outlawing alcohol.

The legislature supported Jim when he wanted free books for children in public schools, more money for rural schools, and a new law to protect tenant farmers. Jim Ferguson was against giving women the right to vote and hold public office, and Miriam agreed with him.

Jim Ferguson won a second term as governor by a wide margin. Miriam must have thought he was popular everywhere, but he wasn't. He had political rivals.

Early in his second term there was talk of impeachment. Jim kept that talk from his family as long as he could. One of the accusations against him was that he spent state money for personal use—household help and groceries for Miriam, cut flowers for the house.

The personal fortune he had gathered was gone. His banks in Temple had failed; he had spent money campaigning, and he had been too busy to manage Miriam's property carefully.

To recover, the governor borrowed money from one bank only long enough to borrow from another. He was digging himself deeper and deeper into trouble. Then an anonymous donor loaned him $156,000 to pay his personal debts. Ouida later insisted that it was a legitimate loan, secured by a valuable black-land farm.

When Jim Ferguson refused to name the source of the money, legislators suspected he had taken the money from the Texas Brewers Association. They thought he supported alcohol sales because he vetoed prohibition.

In impeachment proceedings in state or Federal government, the House of Representatives presents the charges against a public official and then the Senate conducts a trial. An official can be impeached—charged—without being removed from office, if the Senate does not vote to convict. In Jim Ferguson's case, the Senate voted against him.

The final uproar came over the University of Texas. Jim Ferguson vetoed the bill approving money for the university. He was angry because the regents (board of trustees) refused to remove certain faculty members who did not share his attitudes and values. The faculty protested, and Jim made jokes about education and its value.

His homespun humor backfired in this case. He was always considered the adversary of intellectuals because he took the side of "the little people." Now he made that worse. Miriam told him he was foolish to tangle with the university.

The Travis County (Austin) grand jury indicted Governor Ferguson for the misuse of public funds and embezzlement.

The Speaker of the House called a special session, which was not entirely legal. The governor, not the speaker, was supposed to call special sessions. Jim Ferguson called a session to consider the appropriation bill for the university. Once in special session, the legislature turned its attention from the university to the matter of impeachment.

The House of Representatives voted to bring impeachment charges against Jim. They used his vetoes of the university bill and prohibition and his supposedly illegal financial dealings as causes.

The governor tried to protect his family. He refused to let them attend the sessions, although Ouida often snuck into the Senate chambers. She was the first one to bring home the news that the Senate voted to remove him from office.

The vote specified that Jim Ferguson could not again hold public office. Some of his friends in the Senate asked that the decision about future public office be left to the voters. The majority of senators stood firm: Jim Ferguson could not run for "any office of honor, trust, or profit" in the state of Texas.

When money was most scarce on the Bosque County ranch, Miriam Ferguson sold butter and eggs produced at the ranch for extra income.

***

Impeachment and Difficult Times

Miriam immediately began packing. She showed no anger or hurt publicly. Privately she was convinced that politicians had betrayed her family.

The Fergusons did not want to go back to Temple. That was where Jim's failed banks were. People in Temple who had once been their friends now believed that Jim Ferguson had cheated them. Others felt the Fergusons thought too much of themselves, and now they had their comeuppance.

The Fergusons moved to their ranch in Bosque County, near Meridian. Life still wasn't difficult for Miriam. She had a cook, a chauffeur to drive her large

Packard, and their house had electricity. Their rural neighbors had none of those advantages.

Jim was at home in the rural setting. He played his down-home role, and his neighbors liked him. Eventually, however, the family ran out of money. Miriam had to give up luxury after luxury, and she had to start driving her own car.

Then seventeen-year-old Ouida insisted on marrying her longtime boyfriend, George Nalle of Austin. George came from an old and socially prominent Austin family. Ouida was determined. She resisted pleas and tempting offers of alternatives. She could not be dissuaded. The Fergusons had no money for a large wedding, so the ceremony was held in Temple, at the family home, and was nearly over-run with curiosity seekers.

Jim Ferguson ran for president on the American Party ticket in 1920 with William J. Hough from New York as his running mate.

Jim felt that the state's newspapers had treated him unfairly, so he started his own newspaper, the *Ferguson Forum*. He tested the Senate's ruling that he could never hold office by running for governor, but he lost by a large margin.

The Senate ruling did not bar him from holding national office. He ran for president of the United States on the American Party ticket in 1920 but did not win. In 1922 he ran for the U.S. Senate against a Ku Klux Klan candidate. Although it was a close election, he lost again. The "little people"—farmers and small-town citizens—supported him, but Jim was opposed by important politicians and newspapers.

Another race for governor would come in 1924. Jim decided that Miriam should run for governor.

Jim Ferguson did not tell Miriam beforehand when he entered her in the 1924 race for governor. She agreed because he explained that it was a good trick to play on his political foes. Miriam saw it as getting even with the people who had impeached Jim.

Chapter 4

Governor Miriam Ferguson

*****

Miriam began the campaign uncertainly. She liked to stay home; she did not like to be out in huge crowds of people. She didn't like to shake hands with people she didn't know. She didn't like reporters who questioned her. At first she was honest with the reporters because that was her nature. But she felt betrayed when they quoted her. Reporters created the picture of a farm wife, which was not Miriam at all.

Jim told her to act like a farm wife and even to wear a sunbonnet. He told her it was a gimmick to get her in office. Then someone sent her a broom to sweep the Ku Klux Klan away. The broom and the sunbonnet became symbols of her campaign.

Early in the campaign Miriam was introduced first at rallies. She greeted the crowd and then said, "Jim will make the speech." In his speeches, Jim referred to them as "Ma and Pa" Ferguson. He was once again playing his good old boy, down-home role.

Another, less likely story is that reporters gave Miriam the "Ma" nickname because of her initials—Miriam Amanda. The nicknames, Ma and Pa, have stuck through history.

Ouida wrote that she would never have called her mother "Ma" because "it didn't fit her dignity." But the slogan "Me for Ma" eventually won Miriam Ferguson two elections. Her most memorable campaign slogan was "Two Governors for the Price of One."

Jim preached against the Ku Klux Klan, the lack of good highways in Texas, and government that misused the people's money (even though he had been accused of that). Pa claimed that the reason poor people landed in prison was that the government spent

XXX

A woman named Claire Ogden wrote a novel titled The Woman of It, *based on the life of Miriam Ferguson. The novel is not true to the facts of Miriam's life.*

their money. He kept on attacking higher education for wasting money that could be used to teach rural school children.

Suffragists—those who fought for women's rights—were strongly against Ma's candidacy. They thought it was evident that she was running to clear the family name, not to govern the state of Texas. They claimed she would be taking orders from a man who had been anti-feminist when in office. But their campaign did not have any effect.

Miriam changed during the campaign. She became more self-confident. She began to make short speeches about what she believed in. She was strongly in favor of prohibition and education. She was, she said, for higher education but not at the cost of funds for rural schools. She was against the Ku Klux Klan, state spending, and the current prison system. She wanted to improve highways.

She said many of the same things Jim did, but she said them less angrily. And she gave Jim credit for most of her political positions.

Several men ran against her in the primary, but her strongest opponent was Judge Felix Robertson, a member of the Klan. Robertson ran on a ticket of white supremacy and prohibition. He said anyone who didn't agree with him was a lover of Negroes, Jews, foreigners, and Catholics. Judge Robertson won the first primary.

In Texas if no one candidate receives a majority in the first primary, a run-off election is held between the top two candidates. Miriam was by now a much better campaigner and even seemed, according to daughter Dorrace, to be enjoying herself. Some of Jim's old opponents came over to her side because of her stand against the

Klan. And even a few suffragists began to think she might really govern on her own.

Miriam beat Judge Robertson in the second primary and went on to defeat the Republican candidate, a law professor from the University of Texas, by a wide margin.

Ma Ferguson once said, "I love politics. I live it, eat it, and breathe it. Once you get it in your blood, you can't get over it."

She was fifty years old, a typical, middle-class housewife, a little plump and with a little gray in her hair. She had spent only $800 on her campaign.

***

First Term

Miriam Amanda Wallace Ferguson was inaugurated in January 1925. Outgoing Governor Pat Neff introduced her and put aside for the time his dislike of Jim. He left her a picture of Woodrow Wilson, for high ideals and self-sacrifice, a Bible, and a white flower for purity of motives.

On January 20, Governor Ferguson drove her family to the Governor's Mansion in the old Packard in which they had left in disgrace. As she drove up to the house, she said, "Well, we departed in disgrace; we now return in glory."

Governor Miriam Ferguson arrived in her office every morning, worked until noon, returned after lunch and stayed until midafternoon. Then she went home for the afternoon rest she was used to. In the late afternoon she sometimes gardened or worked on papers she had brought from her office. She was very conscientious about her responsibilities as governor.

Jim Ferguson had a desk in his wife's office, right next to hers. He conducted much of the business, while Ma watched. He spoke with visitors, met with the comptroller about the budget, and dealt with legislators.

Miriam believed this fulfilled her campaign slogan about two governors for the price of one. She also liked the fact that she and her husband could be partners in political affairs.

Miriam's most important interest as governor was to restore to Jim the right to hold public office. On February 10, 1926, an amnesty law restored Ferguson's political rights. The Texas attorney general, Dan Moody, was a political opponent of the Fergusons. He declared the law invalid, but the governor signed the bill.

As governor, Mrs. Ferguson was concerned about prisons in Texas. She disliked the cruel treatment and harsh living conditions of the prisoners. She thought minor offenses should be punished with helpful work, such as on road gangs. She thought it wrong to take a man away from supporting his family for violations of the liquor law. It did no good to put a man in prison to sit for two years.

Jim had several convicts brought to Austin to clean up the old military camp, Camp Mabry. Every night the Ferguson family went to eat dinner with the convicts. Jim Ferguson knew they were safe. The convicts would not allow anyone to threaten them. If they did, the entire bunch would be sent back to Huntsville.

During her term, Mrs. Ferguson issued over a thousand full pardons and nearly that many conditional pardons.

Jim Ferguson always said rich, white men did not go to prison, only the poor and the blacks. He began to represent families seeking pardons for loved ones. He charged them for presenting their case to his wife.

The Fergusons were accused of taking money for pardons. The woman who was pardons secretary for Mrs.

The Fergusons' oldest daughter, Ouida, wrote that her mother had unlimited faith in Jim, calling him the greatest lawyer in Texas and a better businessman than any other of his time.

Ma may have been accused of being soft on criminals, but she was particularly interested in catching Clyde Barrow. He was a Texas outlaw and bank robber, best known as half of the Bonnie (Parker) and Clyde team. The movie Bonnie and Clyde *was later made of the couple's adventures and robberies.*

Ferguson said that people brought newspaper-wrapped packages, which Jim Ferguson put in a safe in a basket marked "personal."

Governor Ferguson was even accused of pardoning Klansmen, though this is unlikely. She despised the Ku Klux Klan, and one of her major accomplishments was to pass an anti-mask bill. That made it difficult for the white-robed Klansmen to hold their rallies because they weren't allowed to hide their identity behind masks.

Several railroads hired Jim as general counsel, which could easily have been viewed as a conflict of interest. How could he be a fair advisor to the governor and at the same time a counsel for the railroads? He tried to charge reporters for interviews, although he didn't get far with that.

He asked Miriam to appoint him to the Texas State Highway Commission, and she did. Then he urged companies bidding for contracts to advertise in his newspaper. Soon he was awarding highway contracts as though he alone were the commission.

There were angry accusations that Jim was really the governor, and some politicians called for a special session of the legislature to impeach Ma Ferguson. She refused to call a special session. Jim had been impeached when he called a session, and she knew better.

Miriam was much more social than she had been as the governor's wife, and she opened the mansion to social events. Ouida and her husband, George Nalle, helped with the entertaining.

The Fergusons welcomed various important visitors. Ma served her own chili to Will Rogers, and he entertained the family with stories of the Ziegfeld Follies. Ernestine Schumann-

Heink, the European opera singer, visited them; so did actress Clara Bow, but Ma disapproved of her makeup and the way she sat in the laps of senators.

By the end of her first term, Mrs. Ferguson had dealt with the prisons and the Klan. She had passed a budget she believed used taxpayers' money wisely, and she had provided for the education of rural children. She decided to run again.

Her longtime political opponent, Attorney General Dan Moody, was her strongest challenger. It was a nasty campaign, with many accusations on both sides. Many Ferguson supporters decided to support Moody. He was elected, and Miriam was distinctly cool at the inauguration.

Introducing the new governor, she said, "He was not my choice, but he is yours." What she meant was, since the people had elected him, they would have to put up with his term of office.

Chapter 5

A Second Term and the End of an Era

*****

Jim Ferguson built his family a Mediterranean-style house on Windsor Avenue in west Austin. No one knows who paid for the house, since the Fergusons had no money. But Miriam was able once again to stay at home with her family and her garden.

One of Dan Moody's first acts in office was to repeal the law that would have allowed Jim Ferguson to hold public office again.

Even if Jim Ferguson could not run for office, he could still help candidates he liked. He campaigned for Al Smith, a Catholic from the East who ran unsuccessfully for president. He worked hard for Franklin Delano Roosevelt and for Lyndon Baines Johnson, a young politician who ran for the U.S. House of Representatives. Jim had known the Johnson family a long time.

In 1930, Jim Ferguson persuaded his wife to run again for governor. This time her opponent was oilman Ross Sterling. Miriam shared her husband's dislike of oil, cotton, and lumber millionaires. She won the primary but lost the runoff to Sterling and went back to her house on Windsor Avenue.

Jim persuaded her to run again in 1932. The campaign was ugly. Jim made wild accusations about Sterling's business interests and promised that Ma would lower taxes. There were accusations of illegal votes on both sides. Miriam won the primary and the runoff.

Sterling called for a recount and asked that the state Democratic convention declare the election invalid. When that didn't work, he filed suit in court.

The Great Depression began in 1929 when stock market prices collapsed. Investors were ruined. Banks had no money. Jobs disappeared, and many people went hungry.

For the suit to go to court, Miriam had to be served papers by a certain date. She and Jim began to hide from the process servers who would hand her official papers requiring her presence in court. If she never received the papers, she did not have to be in court.

First they stayed at the Windsor Street house; then they hid at Ouida and George's house near the University of Texas campus. When process servers came to that house, Ouida denied her parents were there. Then the whole family sneaked into a car and headed for the ranch in Bosque County. Miriam thought it was all a great game.

The papers were never served, and Miriam's name was on the state ballot. She was elected.

***

Second Term

Miriam Ferguson was inaugurated for her second term in January 1933. Outgoing Governor Ross Sterling did not attend the ceremony, and his wife did not leave the traditional hot meal for the Fergusons.

But Miriam was pleased that her grandson's Boy Scout Troop was the honor guard. That made the day worth it.

The second term was not much different from the first. Ma replaced Sterling's staff with her own people. Jim had a desk in her office again.

The country was caught in the Great Depression, and it was a difficult time to govern. People across the

President Roosevelt developed government programs which gave people jobs, such as the Civilian Conservation Corps and the Works Progress Administration. Many of the improvements made by these two groups can still be seen today.

country were out of work, hungry, desperate. When banks began to fail nationally, Ma closed the Texas banks for three days to avoid a "run" on the banks where everyone withdraws their money at once and ruins the bank and the economy. She also found federal programs to help people who had lost their jobs.

During her second administration she signed a bill announcing the Texas Centennial celebration in 1936, the 100th anniversary of Texas' freedom from Mexico. Governor Ferguson got the cities of Dallas and Houston to cooperate by promising the Texas Centennial would be held in Dallas and the state Democratic convention in Houston.

Governor Ferguson also signed a bill creating the Lower Colorado River Authority, which built dams on the river and provided electricity to rural families. It was a major accomplishment and a great improvement in the lives of the farmers she and Jim protected.

During her second term in office, Ma Ferguson continued to focus on prison reform. She issued many pardons to convicts, which brought her much criticism. She and Jim again were accused of accepting money for pardons. Nola Woods, the pardons secretary on Miriam's staff, told people that Jim took money. If Jim told Miriam it was all right, she believed him.

Miriam supported the repeal of prohibition because she thought it had been a failure. It didn't stop people from drinking, and it encouraged the illegal sales of alcohol, which made some people rich. It also encouraged people to make homemade whiskey, called moonshine.

She also offended religious groups by helping to legalize horse-race betting at the Arlington Downs and Alamo Downs racetracks in Texas. She even went to the races and placed bets and had a grand time.

W. Lee "Pappy" O'Daniel worked for Burrus Mill and Elevator Company. The company sponsored a radio show and a western music group known as The Light Crust Doughboys to advertise their Light Crust Flour. The most famous "doughboy" was fiddler Bob Wills, who went on to an important musical career.

Miriam Ferguson's second term was a mix of successes and questionable activities. She did not run in 1934 but returned to her home and her garden. She still had her maid and her handyman.

She took a trip to Hollywood where celebrities entertained her. She was invited to the dedication of the Centennial State of Texas Building in Dallas, and Baylor University gave her an honorary degree. She kept up with state and national politics as World War II approached.

Jim always thought Miriam would have a third term. Many Texans, he claimed, wanted her to run again. He himself wanted to run for Congress, but the Fergusons did not have the money for a campaign. Miriam's farm in Bell County had been pledged as security for a loan and was lost.

Miriam was happy staying at home until Pappy O'Daniel, a flour salesman who had a popular radio program, was elected governor in 1938. She did not think a "Yankee" should be governor of Texas. In 1940, she decided to run again. She was sixty-five years old.

Pappy O'Daniel had more campaign money than the Fergusons, and he had important politicians on his side. He survived the Fergusons' insults and political tricks. Miriam came in fourth in the primary. O'Daniel was elected governor.

Miriam went back to Windsor Avenue, but Jim continued to try to influence Texas politics. He disliked Governor O'Daniel and worked to elect him to the U.S. Senate just to get him out of the state. In doing so, he helped defeat his loyal supporter, Lyndon Johnson.

Jim Ferguson worked hard to put Coke Stevenson in the governor's office. His methods were not always honest and open. After Stevenson was elected, he did not have anything to do with the Fergusons.

George Parr was known as the Duke of Duval County (in South Texas). He controlled who held office and, apparently, how people voted. He was a great friend and supporter of the Fergusons and of Lyndon Baines Johnson.

Jim Ferguson had increasing physical problems. He was loosing his hearing, and he didn't have his usual energy. Then an undiagnosed illness caused him to lose a great deal of weight. He suffered a stroke in February 1944 and died September 21, 1944. He and Miriam had been married forty-four years.

Miriam went back to her garden and her grandchildren, but she continued to follow politics. Lyndon Johnson did not hold a grudge about the senatorial race. He visited Miriam often and told her what was going on in the national and state legislatures.

When he ran for the U.S. Senate again in 1948, Ma worked hard to get him elected. She sent letters to her followers and friends and organized a telephone campaign. She did not always treat LBJ's opponent,

Coke Stevenson, fairly. She had pledged to settle the score with Stevenson for his treatment of Jim. When the election seemed to go to Stevenson, Miriam called her friend George Parr, a powerful South Texas political boss in Duval County. Johnson was elected by eighty-seven votes.

Miriam Ferguson never again was active in politics, although she read the newspaper and kept up with her old political friends. She was lonely without Jim and spent a lot of time with his namesake, Dorrace's son Jim. In 1961, she had a heart attack. After that she could no longer work in her garden or leave her house.

Miriam Ferguson died on June 25, 1961. She was eighty-six years old. Her last words were supposedly, "Jim! Jim! Jim!"

Dorrace and her husband, Stuart Watt, and their son Jim, lived with Miriam in the Windsor Street house for ten years. Stuart and Miriam did not get along very well.

Timeline

1875—Miriam Amanda Ferguson born on June 13

1894—Miriam attended Baylor Female College in Belton

1898—Joseph Wallace died

1899—Miriam married Jim Ferguson on December 31

1900—Ouida Ferguson born

1903—Dorrace Ferguson born

1914—Jim Ferguson decided to run for governor of Texas

1915—Jim Ferguson inaugurated as governor

1916—Jim Ferguson re-elected governor

1917—Jim Ferguson was impeached

1924—Miriam Ferguson elected governor

1925—Miriam Ferguson inaugurated in January

1926—Amnesty law restored Jim Ferguson's political rights

1926—Dan Moody beat Miriam when she ran for re-election

1930—Jim Ferguson persuaded his wife to run for governor again; she lost

1932—Miriam ran for governor again and was successful

1934—Miriam did not run for re-election and returned to her garden in Austin and her grandchildren

1940—Miriam ran against Pappy O'Daniel for governor and lost

1944—Jim Ferguson died on September 21

1961—Miriam Ferguson died on June 25 at eighty-six

Glossary

Amnesty—a pardon for offenses against a government

Asthma—a breathing disorder, sometimes severe, often caused by allergies

Black land—the rich black soil found in a wide band across Central Texas; good for farming, as compared to the sandy soil found in other parts of the state

Drought—an unusually long period without rain; sometimes, in Texas, called drouth

Invalid—not valid or well founded; indefensible.

Ku Klux Klan—a national secret organization known for promoting the idea that white people were superior to African-Americans; at their meetings they wore white robes and hoods which hid their faces.

Meningitis—an infection of the membranes around the brain and/or spinal cord

Ratify—to accept or approve, and thereby make legal

Recluse—someone who rarely leaves his or her home or receives visitors

Smallpox—a contagious disease that causes open sores on the skin; possibly fatal; the sores often leaves scars.

Stroke—a rupture of blood vessels in the brain, sometimes causing loss of speech, loss of memory, and/or paralysis. Severe strokes can cause death.

Suffrage—the right to vote, usually applied to women in the nineteenth and early twentieth century

Suffragette—a woman who fought to gain the right to vote for all women

Tenant Farmer—a farmer who works land belonging to someone else and pays the rent with a portion of the crops

Further Reading

Judy Alter. *Extraordinary Women of the American West*. Danbury, CT: Children's Press, 1999.

James M. Day et al. *Women of Texas*. Waco, TX: Texian Press, 1972.

Nelda Patteson. *Miriam Amanda Ferguson: First Woman Governor of Texas: Her Life Story Presented Through the Clothes She Wore*. Women of Texas, Book 2. Smiley, TX.: Smiley & Co., 1994.

May Nelson Paulissen, and Carl McQuery. *Miriam: The Southern Belle Who Became the First Woman Governor of Texas*. Austin, TX: Eakin Publishing, 1995.

Notable American Women: A Biographical Dictionary. 4 Vols. Cambridge, MA: Harvard University Press, 1971-1980.

Ouida Wallace Ferguson Nalle. *The Fergusons of Texas; Or, "Two governors for the price of one," a biography of James Edward Ferguson and his wife, Miriam Amanda Ferguson, ex-governors of the State of Texas*. San Antonio, TX: Naylor Company, 1946.

Ronnie C. Tyler, ed. *The New Handbook of Texas*. Austin: Texas State Historical Association, 1996.

Websites

The best way to find articles about Miriam Amanda Ferguson on the web is to use the Google search engine. Here are a sampling of sites:

www.tsl.state.tx.us/governors/personality/mferguson-p01.html (Texas State Library and Archives Commission photo collection of Miriam Ferguson)

www.twu.edu/firstladies/maw_ferguson.htm (a brief timeline with a discussion of the gown Governor Ferguson wore at her second inauguration)

www.tsha.utexas.edu/handbook/online/articles/FF/ffe6.html

www.historybuff.com/states/tx.html (a list of Texas facts, including governors)

http://en.wikipedia.org/wiki/Miriam_Ferguson

www.heniford.net/1234/3f_smb.htm (a play in which Ma Ferguson appears as one of the characters)

Index